Bear
Sees
COLORS

Karma Wilson

Illustrations by
Jane Chapman

Margaret K. McElderry Books • New York   London   Toronto   Sydney   New Delhi

Mouse and Bear are walking;
they are chitter-chatter-talking.
So much for them to do.
And the bear

sees . . .

blue!

Blue flowers
by the trail.
Blue berries.
Blue pail.

Blue, blue EVERYWHERE!
Can you spy blue with Bear?

Along the trail hops Hare.
"Howdy-ho there, Mouse and Bear!"
Hare points up ahead.
And the bear

sees . . .

red!

Red blossoms.
Red cherries.
Red, juicy
raspberries.

Red, red EVERYWHERE!
Can you spy red with Bear?

Badger's at the pond
with his old galoshes on.
"Look there!" Badger bellows.
And the bear
sees . . .

yellow!

Drippy, sticky,
oh-so-yummy
honeycombs
with yellow honey.

Yellow, yellow EVERYWHERE!
Can you find it, just like Bear?

Gopher's out with Mole.
They are on a little stroll.
Bear spots them by the stream,
and the bear
sees . . .

green!

Green mint
for making tea.
Green and tasty
sweet peas.

Green, green EVERYWHERE!
Can you spy green with Bear?

Raven, Owl, and Wren
lay a picnic in the glen.
The friends all gather round,
and the friends

see . . .

brown!

Chocolate cake,
brown and sweet.
Brown cookies,
such a treat.

Brown eyes,
brown hair.
Friendly, fluffy,
brown . . .

BEAR!

Colors, colors EVERYWHERE!
Can you find colors, just like Bear?

To Emma. Bear and I say thanks.
—K. W.

To Jo, Jeremy, and Charlotte.
—J. C.

THE BEAR BOOKS • MARGARET K. MCELDERRY BOOKS • An imprint of Simon & Schuster Children's Publishing Division • 1230 Avenue of the Americas, New York, New York 10020 • Text copyright © 2014 by Karma Wilson • Illustrations copyright © 2014 by Jane Chapman • All rights reserved, including the right of reproduction in whole or in part in any form. • MARGARET K. MCELDERRY BOOKS is a trademark of Simon & Schuster, Inc. • For information about special discounts for bulk purchases, please contact Simon & Schuster Special Sales at 1-866-506-1949 or business@simonandschuster.com. • The Simon & Schuster Speakers Bureau can bring authors to your live event. For more information or to book an event, contact the Simon & Schuster Speakers Bureau at 1-866-248-3049 or visit our website at www.simonspeakers.com. • Book design by Lauren Rille • The text for this book is set in Adobe Caslon. • The illustrations for this book are rendered in acrylic paint. • Manufactured in China • 1016 SCP • This Margaret K. McElderry Books proprietary hardcover edition November 2016 • 10 9 8 7 6 5 4 3 2 1 • Library of Congress Cataloging-in-Publication Data • Wilson, Karma. • Bear sees colors / Karma Wilson ; illustrations by Jane Chapman. — 1st ed. • p. cm. • Summary: While taking a walk with Mouse, Bear meets many other friends and sees colors everywhere. • ISBN 978-1-4424-6536-7 (hardcover : alk. paper) — ISBN 978-1-4424-6539-8 (e-book) [1. Stories in rhyme. 2. Bears—Fiction. 3. Animals—Fiction. 4. Friendship—Fiction. 5. Color.] • I. Chapman, Jane, 1970– ill. II. Title. • PZ8.3.W6976Bds 2014 • [E]—dc23 • 2012040992 • ISBN 978-1-4814-9507-3 (Raising Readers proprietary edition)

Beyond Reading Aloud

Your little one is so much more aware of the world around us! You may notice your child pointing to things and asking "What's that?" over and over. This is because two year olds are on the very edge of a language explosion. Over the next year, you'll find your little one learns new words at a surprising rate. Even when your child isn't using new words, the "word bank" of words they understand is growing. Books like this one with concept words like colors, help your child to have the language to talk about the world.

Bear Sees Colors
Making Connections

1 Connect to Text:

Play *I Spy* when you read this book with your child. See if your child can find something in the room that is the color mentioned on each page of the book. Work to find several things that are that color.

2 Word Play:

Play the game even when you aren't reading the book. "I spy something RED!" This is a great game for waiting rooms, restaurants, on walks, driving through town, anywhere! If your child points to things that are red, invite him or her to say what they see. You want to encourage your child to use words rather than just pointing.

3 Learn How Books Work:

Point to the words as you read so your child starts to make the connection between what you say and the text on the page. Say, "I'm reading the words on this page."

Find more suggestions at **www.raisingreaders.org**